THE BEST CAMEROONIAN SHORT STORIES

Copyright Information

Website: knowledgeconnectafrica.org
E-mail: info@knowledgeconnectafrica.org

ISBN: 979-8-9907165-0-6

Acknowledgments

We are honored to recognize the remarkable individuals whose expertise and insights have greatly enriched our anthology. Their diverse backgrounds and deep commitment have been instrumental in shaping this project.

NDZEMAMUE MUTUELA SAMUEL

We extend our deepest gratitude to NDZEMAMUE MUTUELA SAMUEL, whose invaluable contributions as an educator, author, and Christian counselor have greatly enriched this collection. His diverse experiences across continents, dedication to bridging cultural divides, and unwavering support for young writers and thinkers in Cameroon have been truly inspirational. We honor his lifelong journey of education which continues to inspire younger generations in Cameroon.

Lilianne MINLO

We extend our sincere gratitude to Lilianne MINLO, whose trailblazing career in journalism and broadcasting has enriched our collection with profound insights. Her expertise, spanning roles from journalist to Editor-in-Chief, has significantly enhanced the depth and authenticity of our narratives. Her insightful feedback on character development and pacing was invaluable in shaping the final stories. We are deeply grateful for her dedication and expertise.

Nkwakeu Pascale AUROLY EPSE TABI

We are immensely grateful to Nkwakeu Pascale AUROLY. A polymath from Cameroon, Nkwakeu's brilliance in public law and linguistics has greatly enriched our project. Her invaluable work as an interpreter and translator has deepened our understanding of diverse cultural narratives. Her guidance as a pastor and counselor reflects her deep commitment to community and spiritual growth. We honor her dedication to fostering intellectual and literary excellence.

Rahael Ngoh Manang

We extend our deepest gratitude to Rahael Ngoh Manang, a beacon of literary brilliance whose work as a writer, editor, and storyteller resonates deeply with the soul of Africa. Her leadership at Inside Consulting and Buma Kor Publishers has enriched our narratives, and her dedication to storytelling and community empowerment exemplifies her transformative impact on African literature, particularly among young writers in Cameroon.

Dr. Solange Swiri Tumasang

Dr. Solange Swiri Tumasang, a luminary in education and sociolinguistics, provided invaluable insights that have enriched our narratives. Her dedication to societal transformation and empowering vulnerable groups through her foundational work in Cameroon and Africa has enhanced the integrity and impact of our collection. We honor her commitment to fostering understanding and advocating for change.

Walter Nwanja

We deeply value Walter Nwanja's pivotal role in our anthology. A passionate advocate for literature, seasoned writer, and experienced self-development coach, Walter's mastery of words enriches our collection. His bilingual proficiency and extensive global experience, including work with the United Nations, provide unique insights that enhance the depth and authenticity of our narratives. We are immensely grateful for his expertise and dedication.

Pride Bih Angu espse Nnamdi

We are profoundly grateful to Pride Bih Angu espse Nnamdi for her critical role in enriching our anthology. Her background in nursing and nutrition, alongside her poetic endeavors—particularly her book "Rays from Above"—has provided unique insights that deeply enhance the authenticity of our narratives. Pride's dedication has been instrumental in showcasing the spirit of Cameroonian literature. We sincerely thank her for her tireless contributions.

We are also indebted to Katherine Oluwakemi Adegoke, Mangwi Ntumngia Fon, Stephanie BIHINA, and Bolanle Akinloye for their meticulous proofreading and formatting efforts, and to Lillian Lippold for her careful proofreading and insightful edits. Their meticulous attention to detail and insightful edits have significantly enhanced the quality of our final manuscript.

Introduction

Cameroon, a country brimming with cultural wealth and diverse traditions, is a wellspring of storytelling. It is within this rich land and culture that Knowledge Connect Africa proudly presents this anthology of short stories.

These tales, selected from our 2023 Writing Summer Campaign, encapsulate the enduring spirit of faith in Cameroon, the vibrance of the nation's culture past and present, and the intricate weave of our many communities.

Our editorial team has carefully crafted these narratives, ensuring clarity and preserving authentic voices; we extend our deepest appreciation for their tireless efforts in shaping this historic collection, a celebration of literary artistry in Cameroon.

The voices in this collection are truly powerful, emotional, and captivating. From the touching diasporic narrative of "Enanga's Journey," to the harrowing yet hopeful tale of "Aïssatou's Path from Adversity to Hope," each story invites us to explore specific and personal facets of life and experience in the country. Stories like "Test of Faith: A Journey to Parenthood" delve into the trials of yearning for divine blessings, while others like "The Cry of a People" poignantly capture more political issues, such as the collective yearning for justice and acknowledgment.

Though beautifully crafted on the page, these narratives are more than just stories. They are crystal-clear windows into the souls of their authors, who offer us their laughter, tears, resilience, and moments of revelation. These authors have generously shared their personal stories, and we are deeply grateful for their contributions to this literary accomplishment.

As this collection takes its first breath in the inaugural edition of our literary series, it is our hope that the anthology will not only honor the writers and their journeys but also echo the voices and heritage of Cameroon at large. In unity and diversity, we present these stories to you: a mosaic of Cameroon's true soul, narrated through faith and shared humanity. We invite you to immerse yourself in their pages.

We look forward to many more projects of this kind, where stories serve as beacons, guiding us towards a future where literature continues to be a cornerstone of our cultural identity.

Rawlings Akondi, Ph.D
Operations Strategist and Contributing Editor
Knowledge Connect Africa Magazine

About the Foreword Author

Dr. Solange Swiri Tumasang is an internationally celebrated educator, researcher, and advocate for social change in Cameroon. Holding a PhD in Sociolinguistics, she is a passionate English language educator and a prolific researcher, with numerous publications and presentations on language acquisition and persuasive discourse.

Dr. Swiri Tumasang is deeply committed to empowering women and children. She founded the Dr. Tumasang Swiri Foundation, Kids for Kids Cameroon, and the Network of Women-Led Civil Society Organizations in Cameroon (NEWOLEC), initiatives that have transformed countless lives through education, mentorship, and advocacy.

A recognized poet and recipient of the 'Best Female Poet' award in Cameroon, Dr. Swiri Tumasang's creative spirit complements her dedication to social justice. Her influence extends globally as a sought-after speaker on women's rights, peacebuilding, and sustainable development.

Named one of the 50 Most Influential Women in Africa in 2024, Dr. Swiri Tumasang is a beacon of progress, inspiring positive change in Cameroon and beyond.

Foreword

Dear Reader,

In this special collection, embark on a remarkable journey through the captivating stories of Cameroon. Inspired by the wisdom and experiences of our diverse and resilient culture, each story in this anthology represents a unique part of Cameroon's cultural heritage, woven together to celebrate the strength, faith, and unwavering spirit of its people. This collection seamlessly integrates into the broader landscape of African literature, enriching it with unique perspectives and narratives. It offers readers a window into the continent's soul through the lens of Cameroon's vibrant traditions and stories.

From "Test of Faith: A Journey to Parenthood," where the human spirit is tested, to the triumphant tales of "An Unexpected Triumph from Adversity" and "Saved by Faith," you will witness the unshakable belief that helps individuals overcome life's challenges. These stories explore the essence of being human, reflecting the struggles, dreams, and longing for justice that are deeply rooted in our nation's soul.

I invite you to delve into this collection, where you will explore the healing power of medicine in "Medicine: Beyond a Vocation" and the depths of faith and spirituality in "Beyond the Veil: A Journey of Spirit and Truth." You will also discover the celebration of Cameroon's diversity in the poetic verses of "Cameroon Blossom and Sacred Thread" and the strength of unity in embracing differences in "Unity in Diversity: Enanga's Cross Cultural Legacy." These stories offer moments of deep reflection, inspiring you to embrace your own story, overcome challenges, and celebrate unity in diversity.

The characters you will encounter in these stories embody the hopes, dreams, and aspirations of our nation, from the trials and triumphs of Aïssatou in "Aïssatou's Path from Adversity to Hope" to the uplifting faith of Benjamin in "The Melody of Benjamin's Faith." These individuals will inspire you, challenge you, and foster a greater sense of compassion and understanding.

By the end of this captivating journey, you will find yourself longing to explore the diverse experiences of Cameroon, often called "Africa in miniature." The pages of this anthology will transport you to a land where culture and tradition intertwine in a mesmerizing dance. You will yearn to explore its hidden corners, experience the bustling marketplaces with their aromatic scents and vibrant colors of traditional garments. The rhythmic beats of traditional music will echo in your ears, connecting you to the primal roots of humanity.

Welcome to the enchanting world of Cameroon, a microcosm of Africa. Welcome to its vibrant cultural diversity, where literature serves as a gateway to enlightenment and transformation. Through this anthology, we not only celebrate the unique essence of Cameroonian culture but also position these narratives as integral to the rich, diverse mosaic of African literature. It's a homage to our shared heritage and an invitation to delve into the complexities and beauties of African stories.

With heartfelt anticipation,
Solange Swiri Tumasang, PhD
Cameroon

Table of Content

Test of Faith: A Journey to Parenthood

By Giborem Coco Nadege

Rain lashed against the taxi window, blurring the vibrant colors of the Bamenda market into a mosaic of hues. Angela sighed deeply, each raindrop a mirror to the tears welling in her eyes.

"Five years," she whispered, the words catching in her throat. "Long years of hoping, praying... waiting."

The steady beat of the windshield wipers echoed the dull ache in her heart. Doctor Ashu's words, though kind, offered no solace. "Healthy," he had said, for the fifth time, "no physical reason why you shouldn't conceive." But his assurances felt hollow, empty promises in the face of her empty womb.

As the taxi pulled up in front of her house in Nghongham, the scent of wet earth and charcoal fires filled the air. Loneliness wrapped around her like a shroud. Sam, her rock, her love, was preparing to leave for Canada. A lump formed in her throat as she thought of facing the empty nights, the silent meals, without him. Her mother-in-law's pointed remarks about her "barrenness" echoed in her ears, a constant reminder of her perceived inadequacy.

Inside, the home was quiet, save for the ticking of the old grandfather clock. Angela's mind raced, excitement bubbling up as she thought of Sam's upcoming birthday. She had been planning a surprise, a small celebration to show him how much she loved and appreciated him. With a renewed sense of purpose, she brushed away her tears and set about tidying up the house.

The next day, with a shopping list clutched in her hand, Angela set off for the Bamenda Main Market. The air thrummed with the energy of the bustling marketplace, the vibrant colors of the fabrics and the enticing aromas of street food momentarily lifting her spirits. She carefully navigated the narrow aisles, dodging wheelbarrows laden with produce and haggling with vendors over the price of spices.

Suddenly, a sharp pain ripped through her abdomen. She doubled over, gasping for breath, her shopping list fluttering to the ground. The world spun into darkness as she collapsed amongst the vibrant fabrics and baskets of plantains.

When she awoke, the sterile scent of the hospital filled her nostrils. Doctor Ashu's face, etched with concern, hovered above her.

"Congratulations, Mrs. Angela," he beamed. "You're pregnant."

Tears streamed down Angela's face, tears of joy, relief, and gratitude. God had not forsaken her. She had been tested, tried, but her faith had endured. Now, she was finally to be blessed with the child she had longed for.

News of the pregnancy spread like wildfire, igniting celebrations in both families. When Sam returned from his trip, his embrace was tighter, his kisses sweeter, than ever before. He held her close, whispering words of love and gratitude into her hair.

Months later, the cries of three healthy babies filled the delivery room. Angela and Sam's hearts overflowed with love and wonder. Their triplets, a testament to their unwavering faith, were a gift from God, a reminder that His timing, though often mysterious, is always perfect. As they held their precious bundles of joy, Angela knew that the years of waiting had not been in vain. They had been a test of faith, a journey that had brought them closer to God and to each other. And in the end, their patience and perseverance had been rewarded with the greatest gift of all - the gift of family.

==

About the Author:

Giborem Coco Nadege, a devoted English language and literature teacher in Cameroon, is a passionate writer who has recently honed her craft under the mentorship of Goodnews Buekor. Her inspiring work includes "Letter to a Pastor's Wife." A wife and mother of three, she balances her dedication to family with her love for teaching and writing.

For further information about her work and to explore collaborative opportunities, Giborem Coco Nadege can be reached at: coconashnkwi@gmail.com

Faith Journey: Overcoming Through Belief

By Penn Elodie Neng

Cameroon, Melody's homeland, is a place where freedom of worship isn't just a right, it's a way of life. "*My kontri don give me plenti chances for show my love for Jesus,*" she declares in Pidgin, her voice a blend of gratitude and conviction. Despite the challenges from non-believers, the nation's unity in faith shines through, like a bright sun on a cloudy day.

Raised in a family where faith was as essential as fufu and eru, Melody was more than a Sunday churchgoer. She sang in the choir, her voice soaring like a bird in the rafters. She volunteered at the orphanage, her heart overflowing with compassion for the children. But even with all this, she sought a deeper connection with God, a thirst that rituals alone couldn't quench. As she matured, so did her understanding of God's light, illuminating her path like the moon on a dark night, revealing her purpose.

"*Your own don too much!*" her parents would tease in Pidgin, amazed by her fervor. But Melody's reply was unwavering: "Trust me, Papa. When you understand Christ, you'll want to get more every day. *E go sweet you for your belle!*"

Yet, Melody's faith was soon to be tested. A health issue plagued her for eight long years: severe menstrual cramps that left her bedridden and often unconscious. The pain was a constant torment, a shadow cast over her once vibrant faith. She would curl up on her bamboo mat, clutching her stomach, tears streaming down her face as she begged God for relief.

"Why me, Lord?" she would cry out. "Haven't I been faithful? Why this suffering?"

Her sister, Mado, noticed her pain during one particularly hard night. Entering the room with a worried look, Mado sat beside her.

"I've been battling these cramps for eight years, Mado. Each episode feels like an eternity," Melody said, her voice weak but filled with a grim determination.

"I've noticed you clutching your faith tighter with each bout. Does it bring you relief, or are you searching for answers?" Mado asked gently, touching Melody's hand.

"It's both. I pray more fervently each time, but I'm not just praying for relief. I'm trying to understand what God wants me to learn from this pain," Melody responded, her eyes reflecting a mix of faith and pain.

"That's what I admire about you, Mel. Even in agony, you look for meaning. But remember, it's okay to ask for help, not just from above but from those around you who care," Mado said, squeezing her hand encouragingly.

Doubts crept in, fueled by the whispers of the enemy. Where was the God she'd trusted so implicitly? Had she done something to displease Him? Was she being punished?

One evening, as Melody lay in agony, Mado rushed in, her face alight with excitement. "Mel, you have to see this!" she exclaimed, pointing to the laptop playing a live stream of a healing service.

Initially skeptical, Melody found herself drawn in by the pastor's powerful words. "Healing is God's gift to the believer," he declared, his voice booming through the speakers. "It is your birthright, your inheritance. Claim it!"

The words struck a chord deep within Melody's soul. Had her healing been hindered not by God's unwillingness, but by her own lack of understanding?

With renewed faith, Melody knelt on the cold cement floor of her room, surrendering her doubts and fears. "Lord, I believe," she whispered, her voice trembling. "I receive your healing now."

The power of God surged through her like a mighty river, washing away the pain and filling her with warmth. The cramps vanished, replaced by a wave of joy so intense, so overwhelming, that she danced around her room, praising God in a mix of English and Pidgin. "Gloryyyyyyyy!! *Papa God, you too much!!*"

Mado rushed in, her eyes wide with amazement. "Mel! You're healed!"

Tears of joy streamed down Melody's face as she embraced her sister, their laughter mingling with sobs of relief.

"Yes, Mado! God has done it!"

Melody's journey, marked by both trial and triumph, is a testament to the power of unwavering belief. It's a reminder that even in the darkest of times, holding onto faith can lead to miraculous breakthroughs.

"All you need to do is just to BELIEVE," Melody affirms, her life a living embodiment of overcoming through faith in God.

About the Author

Penn Elodie Neng, a Law graduate, is a devoted disciple of Christ who excels in story writing and content creation, with a keen eye for detail. Her commitment to exceeding expectations shines in her church and community work. Passionate about spreading the Gospel, advocating for peace, and driving community development, Elodie aims to make a significant impact. With excellent communication skills, she's a valuable leader and team player.

For further information about her work and to explore collaborative opportunities, Penn Elodie Neng can be reached at:

Email: elodiemelodyneng@gmail.com
Facebook: [Elodie Neng]
LinkedIn: [Penn Elodie Neng]
Twitter: [@ElodieNeng]
Instagram: [@elodieneng4]

Penn Elodie Neng is open to inquiries, discussions, and collaborative projects aimed at fostering positive community and national development.

Compromise

By Edna Emade Mesue

As the midday sun cast long shadows over the Presidential visit festivities, Joffi and Kiki navigated through the crowd, immersed in their mission to share the gospel. The vibrant beats of drums filled the air as they moved, their colorful Kabas a stark contrast against the sea of suits and uniforms. Their hands were full of tracts, their hearts imbued with the purpose of spreading the Gospel of Jesus Christ.

A young boy weaving through the crowd caught their attention, expertly balancing a steaming pot of pepper soup on his head. The rich, enticing aroma of spices wafted towards them, momentarily distracting Joffi from her mission.

"Just a taste won't hurt," Joffi suggested, her eyes twinkling with mischief as the boy offered them toothpicks.

Kiki rolled her eyes playfully. "Remember why we're here, Joffi. We have souls to save!"

Joffi grinned, her spirit momentarily lifted by the shared purpose and their deep commitment to their faith. They had walked a considerable distance from Muea, under the relentless February sun, their determination fueled by a desire to make the most of the President's visit to spread the Word of God.

As the day progressed, the vibrant atmosphere intensified. They briefly joined the *Cha Cha* dance; soon, they returned to their primary goal of distributing tracts. The hypnotic *Maley* dance, with its raw cocoyams and live fowls, briefly captivated them, yet they remained focused, slightly bewildered but undeterred in their evangelical mission.

Later, as the sun began to dip toward the horizon, casting an orange glow over the crowd, Joffi found herself drawn away from the festivities. She spotted Tiofack near the food stalls, his face lit by the soft light of early evening. In the calming twilight, his charm seemed more pronounced, lending an intimate quality to their conversation.

Their discussion was lively and full of laughter, but as it drew to a close, Joffi excused herself to rejoin Kiki, who had been patiently waiting nearby. They walked together to a quieter spot near a row of flame trees, where the sounds of the festival were a gentle hum in the background.

"Joffi," Kiki began, her tone layered with a protective edge as they stepped away from the crowd, "be cautious around Tiofack. I can't shake the feeling that his charm masks deeper motives."

"Joffi, still buoyed by the enjoyable interaction, laughed off her concern. "You're overthinking it, Kiki. He's simply being sociable, that's all."

Kiki frowned, her expression one of concern. "I know, but it's more than that. There's something in the way he looks at you... Just be careful, okay? Not everyone's intentions are clear."

After the vibrant *Cha Cha* dance as the sun dipped low, casting long shadows across the festival grounds, Joffi and Kiki made their way to Kiki's aunt's house nestled on the quieter edge of Great Soppo. The warmth and familiarity of the home were a comforting contrast to the day's excitement. In the privacy of a guest room, Joffi slipped out of her colorful *Kaba* and into the red dress, a cherished gift from her late father. The fabric of the dress hugged her, serving as a silent reminder of the strength he had instilled in her. Glancing at her reflection, she steeled herself for the night ahead, the weight of the dress grounding her in the midst of swirling emotions

Excitement fluttered in Joffi's stomach, a nervous energy that buzzed beneath the surface as the festival lights flickered to life.

Each step towards Tiofack's neighborhood felt heavy, the anticipation of the evening a physical weight settling on Joffi's shoulders. The red dress, a silent echo of her father's strength, rustled with every movement, a constant reminder of the values he'd instilled in her.

Joffi found herself standing at Tiofack's doorstep, her heart pounding in her chest. Tiofack's studio was dimly lit, the air heavy with the scent of incense. When he closed and locked the door behind her, a flicker of unease danced in Joffi's eyes.

“Why did you lock the door?" Joffi asked, her voice trembling slightly despite her attempt to sound casual.

"To ensure our privacy, my dear," Tiofack replied, his smile not quite reaching his eyes. "We wouldn’t want any interruptions while we explore your fascinating insights," he added, his tone too smooth, too rehearsed.

As Tiofack's compliments grew increasingly personal, Joffi’s initial flattery turned into discomfort. The sweet scent of incense, once soothing, now seemed to cloud her senses—making it hard to think clearly.

Ignoring the unease, Joffi focused on Tiofack's words, his compliments as sweet as the pepper soup she had tasted earlier. Your faith is truly inspiring, Joffi,' he said. 'I've never met anyone who speaks of God with such conviction. It makes me wonder what other hidden depths you possess.'

As the night wore on, Tiofack's compliments grew bolder, his touch more lingering. The initial thrill of his attention turned to a sickening unease in the pit of Joffi's stomach. Just as Tiofack leaned in, his lips hovering inches from hers, a loud banging on the door shattered the illusion.

The abrupt intrusion into their private world jolted her back to reality. In that heart-stopping moment, Kiki's words echoed in Joffi's mind, a warning bell ringing in her ears. Suddenly, she saw Tiofack for what he truly was: a predator, his charm a carefully crafted facade. She scrambled away, her heart pounding in her chest as she fumbled for the doorknob.

Joffi emerged from the stifling studio, the cool night air a welcome relief. The red dress, once soft against her skin, now felt rigid, a protective armor woven from her father's lessons. His words, once distant echoes, now thundered in her ears, guiding her towards safety.

Dimly lit streets stretched before her, each shadow a lurking threat. Suddenly, a figure emerged—Kiki!

"Joffi!" Kiki cried out, her voice filled with relief and worry. "Are you alright?"

Joffi collapsed into Kiki's arms, tears streaming down her face. "I almost fell," she sobbed, the weight of her near transgression heavy on her shoulders.

Kiki held her friend close, offering words of comfort and reassurance. "Remember who you are, Joffi. God protected you tonight. Hold on to your faith, and you will always find your way back."

After escaping the oppressive atmosphere of Tiofack's studio, each breath of cool night air felt like a cleanse, washing away the remnants of deceit. Joffi's mind was a whirl of emotions as she walked beside Kiki, whose presence was a tangible reminder of the strength of friendship and faith. 'Tonight's trials have taught me the true meaning of vigilance and strength,' Joffi reflected, the lessons of the evening etching themselves deep within her. With each step towards safety, her resolve solidified—fortified by the night's harrowing experiences and the unwavering support of her friend."

As they approached Kiki's aunt's house, Joffi gently traced the fabric of her red dress, now a symbol of her resilience. Each thread seemed to carry the echoes of the night's lessons, weaving her father's wisdom with her own newfound strength. The distant drums of the Maley dance merged with the night's whispers, mirroring the rhythm of her reinforced spirit and reminding her that her faith and friendships were lights guiding her through any darkness.

About the Author

Edna Emade Mesue, a passionate social entrepreneur from the Southwest Region of Cameroon, is dedicated to driving positive change in her community. Edna combines her love for poetry, media, and communication to create innovative solutions that address pressing social issues. Edna is always looking for new opportunities to collaborate and create positive change.

For further information about her work and to explore collaborative opportunities, Edna Emade Mesue can be reached at: ednamesue@gmail.com.

An Unexpected Triumph from Adversity!

By Foncham Precious Andin

The news of her parents' death crashed over Jomia, leaving her lost in a sea of grief. Uprooted from her familiar world at the tender age of twelve, she found herself in the unfamiliar embrace of her maternal aunt's home in the serene village of Bali Nyonga.

Village life, a stark contrast to the vibrant chaos of her former home, demanded adaptation. Jomia rose before dawn, her small hands gripping the cool clay pot as she fetched water from the stream, the cool liquid sloshing against her bare legs. She learned to grind millet and cassava for the communal meals, the rhythmic pounding a soothing counterpoint to her turbulent emotions. Amidst her aunt's six daughters, Jomia found her place as a quiet observer, seeking refuge in books and knowledge.

Her academic prowess was a beacon in the darkness of her grief. She devoured books with a hunger that seemed to fill the void left by her parents. By fifteen, she had achieved an impressive 18 points on her GCE Ordinary Level, a testament to her resilience and intellect. But her dreams of further education were soon extinguished, replaced by the harsh realities of servitude within her aunt's household. The weight of her loss pressed down upon her, and in her darkest moments, she wished for vengeance or a reunion with her parents in death.

Then came the whispers, seeping into her consciousness like a noxious vapor. Whispers of a man from Limbe, a man named Bobgha, who had been promised Jomia's hand in marriage years ago by her aunt. A promise made in the wake of her parents' death, a promise Jomia had no say in. Her heart hammered in her chest, palms slick with sweat as the inevitability of her fate loomed closer.

One afternoon, a sense of foreboding hung heavy in the air, thick as the smoke from the cooking fires. Jomia's aunt summoned her, her voice sharp and urgent. Jomia's stomach churned as she entered the dimly lit hut, the scent of palm oil and wood smoke thick in her nostrils. Her aunt and three other women sat in silence, their faces marked with grim determination. The rhythmic beat of a distant drum pounded in Jomia's ears, each thud echoing the dread that filled her soul.

The women's eyes followed Jomia's every move as she was instructed to lie on a woven mat. A wave of nausea washed over her, but she obeyed, her body rigid with fear. The women's hands, rough and calloused, reached for her. Jomia squeezed her eyes shut, her breath coming in ragged gasps as a searing pain ripped through her. Her cries were muffled by a cloth pressed against her mouth, her body trembling as the agonizing ritual continued.

Shortly after, Jomia was sent to Limbe to live with Bobgha. His house, a dilapidated structure with peeling paint and broken windows, was a shell devoid of warmth or comfort. The morning of her departure was cloaked in an uneasy silence. Jomia packed the few belongings she had into an old, worn-out suitcase, her movements mechanical. As she folded each garment—a mix of hand-me-downs and simple dresses—a tightness gripped her chest, her breath growing shallow with each passing mile.

The journey to Limbe was long and tiresome. Jomia sat in the back of an old bus, the engine groaning as it maneuvered the winding roads edged by lush greenery. Her stomach knotted with each lurch and bump, mirroring the anxiety that twisted within her.

Upon arriving in Limbe, the air was thick with the salt of the sea and the buzz of coastal life, a stark contrast to the quiet village she had left behind. Bobgha was there to meet her at the bus station—a tall, broad-shouldered man whose stern face softened momentarily into a fleeting grin when he saw her. Jomia's apprehension deepened as she followed him to his home, the suitcase handle digging into her palm.

One evening, as the sun painted the sky in fiery hues, Bobgha's temper burned hotter. The fufu was too thick, the vegetables undercooked. A storm of insults filled the small room, his voice a thunderclap shattering the fragile peace. Then came the back of his hand across her face, the sharp sting radiating through her cheek, a dull ache settling in as she stumbled backward.

Fleeing from the oppressive atmosphere of the house, Jomia sought refuge at the beach. As she stepped onto the cool, damp sand, the narrative tempo changed to match the tranquility of the seaside. The waves gently lapped at the shore, each one whispering of release and peace. "Each wave seemed to wash away a layer of fear, drawing out the poison of years spent in silent acquiescence," the story reflects, allowing readers to feel Jomia's relief and gradual easing into a state of reflection. This moment on the beach was her sanctuary, a place where the turmoil of her domestic life receded with the tides, leaving her space to breathe and contemplate her next steps.

In this serene environment, her thoughts slowly untangled, and she could think about her future with more clarity. It was here, with the rhythmic sound of the ocean filling the background, that Jomia found the courage to envision a life beyond her current sufferings. This transition was not just a physical escape from her immediate dangers but also a pivotal moment in her emotional recovery, marking the beginning of her path toward healing and eventually leading to her empowerment and advocacy.

As she stood at the water's edge, tears streaming down her face, a voice broke through her despair. "Child, are you alright?"

Jomia turned to see a woman approaching, her face lined with concern. She was Esther, a teacher at the local school who often strolled along the beach after her day's work. She had witnessed Jomia's distress from afar and felt a motherly instinct to intervene.

Esther listened patiently as Jomia poured out her heart, her words tumbling over each other in a desperate torrent. She offered her comfort and a safe haven, inviting her to her modest home. There, she shared with her the teachings of Christianity, the stories of love, forgiveness, and redemption resonating deep within her wounded soul.

Esther's voice was soft as she spoke, "It takes courage to share one’s pain, Jomia. You’re not alone anymore." They sat under the cool shade of a palm tree, the gentle breeze offering a small respite from their heavy conversation.

Under Esther's nurturing guidance, Jomia began to confront her past traumas more openly. Nights spent under the vast African sky, Esther listening intently, Jomia delved into the darker corners of her heart. "I feel like I'm standing at the edge of a precipice, unsure if my next step will bring a fall or a flight," Jomia confessed one evening. Esther's response was a gentle nod, "Healing is like the new moon, barely there but growing fuller with time." These conversations, rich with metaphor and empathy, charted Jomia's journey from a bruised soul to a beacon of hope.

With each passing day, the bond between them strengthened, and Jomia's faith in her ability to heal and change her destiny grew. This ongoing support and understanding provided by Esther were pivotal in transforming Jomia's outlook on life and her role in it.

With newfound strength and Esther's support, Jomia dared to dream again. Her deepest desire was to explore the wonders of her homeland, a land she had barely known. Together, they embarked on a transformative journey through Cameroon, from the ancient Bamoun Palace with its intricate carvings and colorful tapestries to the pristine beaches of Kribi, where the warm sand met the turquoise waters. Each step reinforced her resilience.

As Jomia's personal healing blossomed into a broader mission, she took her message to the community. "Because of our collective efforts, two neighboring villages have pledged to reevaluate their customs involving women,"

Jomia announced to the gathered crowd, a mix of nervous and proud. The mayor stepped forward, adding, "And thanks to Jomia's bravery, our council is drafting proposals to protect our daughters legally." The camera pulls away from the emotional scene, showing a wide shot of the community clapping, faces alight with the dawn of change, signaling not just Jomia's personal victory but a communal triumph.

This odyssey of self-discovery, laughter, and growth ignited a passion within Jomia to share her story. She poured her experiences into the pages of her memoir, *Rising from the Ashes*, a testament to her transformation from victim to victor, from despair to faith. Her words, like the rhythmic drums of her homeland, echoed her unwavering spirit, a reminder that even in the darkest of nights, hope can always be found.

About the Author

Foncham Precious Andin is a Cameroonian menstrual activist and founder of Societal Elevators, an organization promoting menstrual health education and advocacy. She empowers women and girls through workshops and her YouTube channel, "Get Impeccable." Precious also volunteers with the DeWise Foundation, supporting internally displaced persons in Cameroon. A talented writer, she crafts short African stories celebrating women's resilience and exploring themes of empowerment, cultural identity, and social justice.

She can be reached through email at preciousandin1@gmail.com, on Facebook as Precious Andin Foncham, on YouTube at Get Impeccable, and on LinkedIn as Precious Andin Foncham.

Medicine: Beyond a Vocation

By NGOHOBA Vigny Sayal

(This article was originally submitted in French))

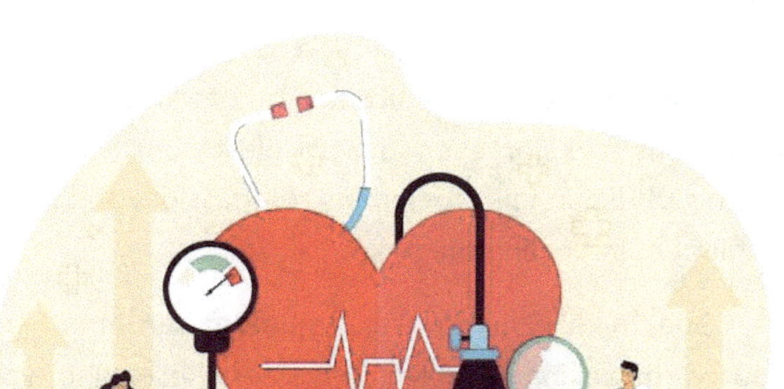

After completing his medical studies, Kevin Meyong, a young man eager to gain professional experience, relocated to the bustling city of Ebolowa. He had secured a position at the local medical center and found a modest studio apartment in the vibrant New Bell neighborhood. There, he quickly befriended Gerold and Carol Fuh Mbang, a young couple from the Southwest Region who had moved to Ebolowa with dreams of successful poultry farming. However, the harsh economic realities had forced them to seek alternative sources of income. Carol sold cassava fritters by the roadside to supplement her husband's meager earnings from carpentry work. The couple shared their living quarters with a mysterious young woman named Rose Mayembe, whose door always remained closed.

Kevin soon gained a reputation in the neighborhood for his selfless generosity and willingness to help anyone in need, regardless of their ability to pay. This baffled many of his neighbors, who were accustomed to doctors charging exorbitant fees for even the simplest consultations. But Kevin's Christian faith fueled his compassion, and he found fulfillment in healing the sick.

One night, a heated argument erupted in the courtyard, waking Kevin from his sleep. Rose, who typically kept to herself, was embroiled in a fierce dispute with Carol over Rose's loud music after returning from one of her late-night outings. Kevin intervened, calming the situation and escorting Carol back to her apartment, as Gerold was away for the night.

The following morning, as Kevin prepared to attend his usual Sunday church service, he encountered Rose in the courtyard, hanging her laundry. "Oh, look at you, Mr. Pious, with your big Bible," Rose scoffed, her voice dripping with sarcasm. Kevin smiled gently. "When I return, I'll share the sermon with you," he replied, unfazed by her cynicism.

"Spare me the lecture," Rose retorted dismissively.

Carol emerged from her apartment, hurling insults at Rose, accusing her of being a prostitute. Sensing another imminent confrontation, Kevin intervened once again, leading Carol back inside. This detour caused him to miss his church service, giving him an unexpected opportunity to approach Rose. He knocked on her door, and she opened it, her expression guarded. Kevin spoke softly, explaining that he understood her resentment but wished she knew him better.

Rose scoffed, not even bothering to look at him. "All those churchgoers are hypocrites," she spat. "They call me a prostitute, but it's the elders, pastors, and so-called saints who come to me in secret. It's their money that furnished this apartment."

Kevin listened patiently, nodding in understanding.

Rose continued, her voice filled with bitterness. "And there's more. Gerold and I are involved. He gives me 30,000 FCFA every month, even though he tells Carol he can't afford to provide for their family. But you have to keep it a secret; he's a violent man."

Kevin remained silent for a moment, then asked gently, "Do you know that Jesus is alive?"

Rose's anger flared. "You haven't been listening to a word I've said!" she shouted, pushing Kevin out of her apartment.

Days later, on his way to work, Kevin noticed Rose's door ajar, an unusual sight during weekdays. Concerned, he went inside and found her unconscious on the floor, her belongings gone. He rushed her to the clinic, where he treated her and covered all the medical expenses.

When Rose awoke from her coma, she broke down in tears, revealing that the pastor's wife had attacked her with the help of some men because Rose had been involved with the pastor. The wife, who worked at the police station, ensured that Rose couldn't file a complaint. As she sobbed, Kevin shared the message of God's love and forgiveness, offering comfort and solace.

For the first time in her life, Rose was moved by the gospel. She confided in Kevin, explaining that her loneliness and lack of options had led her to prostitution, causing her to drop out of university. Kevin, touched by her vulnerability, introduced her to a former patient who owned a restaurant, securing Rose an apprenticeship as a chef.

Meanwhile, Carol's suspicions about Gerold's infidelity grew. Late at night, she lay awake, the glow of Gerold's phone casting shadows across their bedroom. With each message she read, a piece of the life she thought they built crumbled away. Tears streamed silently down her cheeks as she wrestled with the betrayal. Heartbroken and determined, Carol hatched a plan. The following morning, after Gerold left for work and their daughter went to school, Carol prepared a large pot of Eru, a traditional Cameroonian stew, lacing it with rat poison. She intended to offer it to Rose as a gesture of goodwill for her newfound change in behavior, but Rose was already at work. Carol resolved to give it to her in the evening, after returning from her fritter-selling rounds.

Fate, however, had other plans. A power outage at the workshop forced Gerold to return home early. Drawn by the enticing aroma of the Eru, he devoured a large portion.

When Carol returned from school with their daughter, she found Gerold unconscious on the floor. Panicked, she immediately called Kevin, who arrived with Rose. Realizing the gravity of the situation, they prayed fervently over Gerold, who miraculously began to vomit the poisoned food. He regained consciousness, and a tearful Carol confessed her actions.

Rose and Gerold apologized to Carol, and Carol, in turn, apologized to Rose. The entire family, moved by the power of forgiveness, was baptized and eventually saved enough money to revive their poultry farm. Rose continued her culinary training at the restaurant, her life transformed by Kevin's compassion and faith.

The doctor's unwavering belief in God's love had healed not only the physical ailments of his community but also the wounds of their souls. This community transformation, marked by a Sunday service under the trees, was not just a gathering but a celebration of renewed faith, trust, and hope, encapsulating the essence of their collective journey.

About the Author

NGOHOBA Vigny Sayal is a Cameroonian biochemistry doctoral candidate and a rising star in science communication. His unique ability to bridge the gap between scientific understanding and spiritual insight is evident in his writing, which explores the complexities of the natural world through a spiritual lens. Fluent in both French and English, Vigny is passionate about making science accessible and engaging for diverse audiences. He is actively involved in research and is always seeking new opportunities to share his knowledge and passion for science.

To learn more about Vigny's work and explore potential collaborations, you can connect with him via email at vignyngohoba@gmail.com or through his social media profiles on Facebook and LinkedIn.

The Cry of a People

By Madjoufan Kapawou Innette

(This poem was originally submitted in French)

Voices rise in tumult,
Echoing pain, profoundly heard.
A people's outcry soars to heavens,
Manifesting deep-seated unease.

Endless years of anguish, which never cease,
But masquerade as benevolent aid,
Guiding this populace to voice their despair,
Shouting a freshly awakened pain.

Bloodshed marks anguish,
The futile endeavors of valiant souls.
In blood, they waged battles,
Yet their cries fell upon deaf ears at home.

Usurpers took our throne
And drank deep from the king's chalice,
Enslaving our kin, and yet,
Hailed as most valiant warriors.

This people boast an epic tale
Which single lifetime cannot recount.
Every nation basks in a moment of glory,
A defining chapter in a homeland's saga.

Ours, Cameroon, by fate,
We must choose to amplify its cry,
Louder, stronger, we must yell,
Breaking free from wrath entire.

As the end times approach,
Those once-dreaded empires
Begin their final descents,
Leaving but whispers of their past.

Against the resilience of these men,
They falter.
They attempt to exhaust our spirit,
Unaware we're sheltered by a greater force.

The people rise and defend their ground.
For too long they've trodden these paths,
And with each step taken towards perceived finality,
Found themselves more adrift than before.

NO! Those days are now behind!
For amidst the tumult,
We've discovered THE voice!
We've found THE path!

The voice.
The voice of He in whom we trust.
The voice of the highest sovereign.
The voice which empowers the feeble.

Beneath His shelter, we stand.
His hand extends to those who crown Him king.
He who envisions our future,
bestows upon the people their rightful inheritance.

Awaken, O Earth!
Shake off your fears.
You've long been swayed by vile deceivers,
Succumbing to the honeyed words of strangers.

Fortune favors you now,
Blessed with the finest treasures.
Yet, those deceivers wish for your silence,
For your voice to fade.

Is it envy? Perhaps despair?
Fear? Disarray?
Will they attain their goal?
Succeed in ensnaring an entire people?

Their victory hinges on your compliance.
You follow their war tactics,
Seduced, lured by the exotic.

This is an enchanting siren, yes,
With a tongue that weaves tales.
A siren whose sway is the mightiest.
A siren whose blood clamors for retribution.

This is the tale of a woman consumed by spite,
A heart void of compassion.
A deceiver of the wicked,
And thus elevated within their ranks.

The architect of vice,
The seductress,
The initiator,
Seeking to topple those adorned by Elijah's mantle.

You, swayed by her charms,
lose all semblance of your reason.
You are reduced to mere puppets,
Automatons crafted by many hands.

You've become unrecognizable,
Stripped of your truest essence,
Your identity usurped,
Robbed of authenticity.

The puppeteers, from their shadowed seats,
Observe and adjust.
They manipulate each step,
Trigger mechanisms for more destruction.

Together, they push you to the brink,
Casting doubt upon your moral compass,
Asking you to forsake it, finally,
So they may mold you into their desired form.

What remains of your essence?
Are your dreams crushed beneath their heels?
Has the allure of tainted wealth clouded your judgment?
Or in silence, do you still nurse your regrets each day?

Yet, a chance remains!
The final one!
Your last bid for resistance,
Your ultimate stand against this cruelty.

Choose your joy!
Choose your peace!
Choose your happiness!
Choose! Use that choice!

This truth we must forge lies ahead,
The truth that will liberate our nation,
The truth that will uplift our people,
The truth that will extricate us from dominion.

By blood, we shall prevail, but not just any.
The blood of the One who orchestrated all,
The blood of the One who sacrificed life,
The blood of the One who paid the ultimate price.

The Lamb slain,
The valiant warrior,
The soldier supreme,
The keeper of our collective fate.

Without You, how would we bear to endure?
Your strength holds us up through it all.
For You are the key,
Our sole path to liberation.

You endow us with the fortitude to resist the stranger's clasp,
To withstand the allure of her whispers.
You raise us up to proclaim Your mission,
Strengthening our very foundations as you do.

We have foundations of a people poised for their final battle,
A people ready to die in Your glory.

We have the bedrock of seasoned warriors,
Witnesses to a formidable enemy's downfall.

This people, they cry out.
They thirst for justice,
Long for You,
Yearn to celebrate their true King.

This people, their roar for vengeance echoes.
Anguish pours forth, all the way to the throne.
With all their might,
They scream their truth and belief.

We seek Your support.
Together, we crave Your presence,
Knowing, without You, we are nothing.
Without You, we stand no chance.

This world is ripe for revival.
This world calls us to stand as sentinels,
To declare the supremacy of the living God,
And, like the twenty-four elders, to glorify Him without ceasing.

This fading world
Needs lovers of Christ desperately.
We are an army of valiant soldiers,
All willing to sacrifice our lives for His eternal glory.

About the Author

Madjoufan Kapawou Innette is a young Cameroonian writer and avid reader, passionate about the power of words to evoke emotions and breathe life into stories. Her love for language is evident in her evocative writing style and her belief that "writing is not just a passion but a lifestyle." Innette is dedicated to honing her craft and sharing her unique perspective with the world.

For inquiries or collaborations, you can reach her at innettemadjoufan@gmail.com.

Ali's Secret

By Fulbertor Lamba

(This article was originally submitted in French)

At last! The truth had finally come to light. The room buzzed with a few sounds, punctuated by jokes from the class clowns who all sat in the back. Even the professor had fallen silent and was observing the scene unfold. After all, it was his lecture on languages and cultures that had stirred this commotion in the first place.

Ali felt isolated in unfamiliar territory. Suddenly, everyone seemed to be noticing signs that had always been there—his subdued complexion and that distinctive "r" accent—and interpreting them as an identity card for him being of "The North". The room suddenly felt stifling, and all he could do was stand there and endure his tormentors' scrutiny.

The break in class finally came, a reprieve from this nightmare.

"You may leave!" announced the professor. "We will continue after the break..."

Ali began to pack his things, while also being patted irregularly by the crowd which passed by. He heard insults flung carelessly at him,

"Northern SHEEP!"

Upon leaving the room, Ali was approached by Vannelle, one of his classmates. She was a girl of openness, armed with great courage and a big heart.

"Hi!" she said, cheerful. "You must know me. We sit in the same row..."

"Have you also come to mock me?"

"No, why would you say that?" She looked concerned that he'd even say such a thing. "I just wanted to say that I think what's happening to you is partly your own fault."

Ali narrowed his eyes in frustration. "What do you mean? It's them who are mocking me!"

She looked Ali in the eyes, and they began to walk slowly to the cafeteria together. She adopted a more serious and gentle tone.

"Why do you think they're mocking you?"

"Because I'm from the North," he said, matter of fact. "They must hate me."

"Since when is being from the North an insult?" she said, as though he was being ridiculous. "In my opinion, you feel the same way as they do; you both have complexes. Otherwise, you would have behaved differently and wouldn't have been affected by mere words alone."

"Wow..." he stared off in front of him. "I have nothing to say to that."

They stopped just in front of the cafeteria. Vannelle smiled for a moment when they were still. She had found a willing listener to what the majority would never want to hear from her: the truth. He did seem like a truly open-minded individual.

"You're Christian, aren't you?" she asked.

"Yes, but how do you know? People from my region are generally Muslim." This girl really was something special.

"You know, a Christian doesn't hide. That's how it is with us. God really makes us capable of learning new things, forgiving, being tolerant...but I'm going to tell you something important that my mother told me this morning during our meditation."

He tilted his head. "What's that?"

"Love! That's the most important thing." She had a big smile on her face as she spoke. "The Bible tells us to love one another. For now, that's all you need to know to get through what's happening in class. I think, above all, we need to love each other. You must love both yourself and your culture!"

"I see." It made sense to him, and he gave her a smile in return. "You're right! I'll make an effort in that direction."

She nodded in approval. "Next, you need to love others. I'll make this one easier for you: you should try to get to know them, put yourself in their shoes, and understand what they're going through. So, I suppose I can now ask the question again: why are others mocking you?"

"Because they don't know me," he said with a sigh. "Before talking to you, I thought you were like them, but you aren't. So they must also be different when you get to know them. Thank you for this!"

She beamed with pleasure.

Ali's eyes widened. "Let me get you something special! As a thank you."

Vannelle smiled in surprise. "Oh really? What's it?"

Ali led Vannelle to a stand made of old metal sheets. He then ordered two bowls of a special porridge. Vannelle cradled the bowl in her hands and then took a small sip. Her face lit up.

"Hmm! This is the best porridge I've ever tasted!" she exclaimed. "How come I'm only trying it now?"

Ali smiled proudly. "It's a special dish from our region in the North, made with peanuts!"

He then turned to the vendor and the two of them spoke in his local language, Fulfulde. Vannelle watched as the vendor handed Ali two more bowls.

Just then, Ali noticed several of his classmates at the stand. Vannelle didn't hesitate to proclaim far and wide that this porridge was a recipe from the North. She praised the merits of a delicious recipe from that famous region none of them had visited. Ali's smile stretched from ear to ear. He knew her game, and he appreciated her support.

Back in class later that day, the Professor continued the lesson on languages and culture. After a while, he asked Ali to name some typical dishes from his region. Ali stood with a confident smile and a playful demeanor. He was much more relaxed than he'd been before the break.

"First of all," he said, "I'll mention the famous Northern Porridge..."

Everyone burst into laughter, but this time, it was different! It was a laughter of support. The professor was a bit lost as to how things could change over just one break period, but he was happy about it as well. A meal was always a great place for unity to begin.

==

About the Author

Yavee Lamba Fulbert is a Cameroonian veterinary medicine student in Ngaoundéré with a passion for storytelling. He is the author of an unpublished book and a freelance writer, crafting compelling stories and screenplays for film. Yavee's dedication to both veterinary medicine and creative writing showcases his diverse talents and his commitment to making a positive impact through his work. He aspires to inspire and uplift others through his narratives, whether focused on animal welfare or human experiences.

You can connect with Yavee via email at fulbertorlamba@gmail.com or on Facebook as Fulbert Yavee.

Witness to Independence

By Konde Odette Mémoire Céleste

(This article was originally submitted in French)

The air hung heavy with the scent of roasting plantains and the earthy aroma of sweat as I jostled through the crowded marketplace, my schoolbooks clutched tightly against my chest. The vibrant colors of the fabrics swirled around me, a kaleidoscope of patterns and textures that reflected the rich diversity of our land. Yet, beneath this vibrant facade, I could sense a growing unease, a simmering discontent that mirrored my own inner turmoil.

I had always been a quiet observer, content to watch the world unfold from the sidelines. But today, a spark of defiance flickered within me, ignited by the impassioned words of a man named Ruben Um Nyobè.

At the Fulassi Normal School, nestled in the heart of Bulu country, Ruben had been a force of nature, a whirlwind of ideas and unwavering conviction. I recall the hushed whispers that followed him through the halls, the way his voice boomed with righteous anger as he challenged the school's administration, their faces contorted in a mixture of fear and fury. His expulsion did little to quell his spirit; instead, it fueled his determination to fight for a free and independent Cameroon.

Now, as a teacher in Yaoundé, I found myself caught in the crosscurrents of change. The rhythmic beat of the drums, once a joyous celebration of our heritage, now carried a message of defiance. The tantalizing aroma of grilled fish from roadside stalls mingled with the acrid smell of burning tires, a testament to the growing unrest in our streets. The name "Um Nyobè" echoed through the city, whispered in hushed tones in the marketplace, scrawled in bold letters on walls, a symbol of hope and resistance.

One evening, as the sun dipped below the horizon, casting long shadows across our humble courtyard, my mother's voice, usually so gentle and soothing, took on a conspiratorial tone. "There's a man in Edea," she whispered, her eyes gleaming with a newfound fire, "a man who speaks the truth that others dare not utter."

The news spread like wildfire, a spark that ignited a blaze of hope in our hearts. We gathered in secret, our voices hushed yet resolute, as we listened to smuggled recordings of the man's speeches. His words painted a vivid picture of a Cameroon free from the chains of colonialism, a nation where our voices would be heard, our destinies shaped by our own hands.

"Ruben, how do you keep fighting when everything seems against us?" I had once asked during one of those rare, quiet moments we shared away from the eyes of the colonizers.

He looked at me, his eyes alight with an unquenchable fire, "Because our cause is just, and our spirits are unbreakable. And because people like you carry the flame. Don't ever let it go out, not when so many are counting on us to light the way."

In the sweltering heat of April 1948, the UPC (Union des Populations du Cameroun) was born, a union of diverse voices united in their quest for freedom. Ruben, the firebrand of our movement, stood tall at its helm, his eloquence and unwavering conviction electrifying the masses. But the French colonizers, threatened by this burgeoning movement, unleashed a wave of violence upon us, their batons raining down on peaceful protesters, their bullets piercing the air, shattering the fragile illusion of peace.

Newspapers like "The Voice of the People" became our weapon, their pages filled with stories of injustice and calls for unity. But the fight for freedom was not without sacrifice. Clashes with the colonial forces escalated, leaving a trail of bloodshed and sorrow. Ruben, our fearless leader, was forced to flee, his whereabouts shrouded in secrecy.

One scorching afternoon in Bassa'a country, the familiar chant of "Um Nyobè! Um Nyobè!" erupted from the crowd, a tidal wave of sound that washed over me, sending shivers down my spine. I followed the throng to the public square, my heart pounding in my chest.

The scene that greeted us was one of unspeakable horror. Ruben's lifeless body lay in the dust, his once proud form desecrated by the cruelty of his oppressors. A collective gasp swept through the crowd, followed by an eerie silence, broken only by the sobs of mourners.

As I stood there, staring at the lifeless body of my hero, I felt a surge of rage, a burning desire for revenge. But then, I remembered Ruben's words, his message of hope and unity. I knew that violence would only perpetuate the cycle of oppression. Our fight for freedom had to be one of peace, of resilience, of unwavering faith in our cause.

On January 1, 1960, the bells of freedom finally rang throughout Cameroon, their joyous peals echoing across the land. I stood in the crowd, tears streaming down my face, as the tricolor flag of our new nation was raised high. It was a moment of triumph, a testament to the indomitable spirit of our people.

But our journey was far from over. The scars of colonialism ran deep, and the task of rebuilding our nation was daunting. Yet, we were determined to forge a new path, a path guided by the principles of unity, equality, and justice.

Today, as we celebrate Bilingualism Day, a day dedicated to honoring Ruben Um Nyobè's vision of a united Cameroon, I am reminded of the sacrifices made by countless heroes who fought for our freedom. Their legacy lives on, inspiring us to build a nation where all voices are heard, where all dreams are possible.

About the Author

Konde Odette Mémoire Céleste is an inspiring Cameroonian writer whose narratives delve into the heart of human experiences, reflecting the rich cultural tapestry of her homeland. Her work serves as a beacon of inspiration, illuminating the diverse facets of life, love, and resilience. With a passion for storytelling and a deep connection to her roots, Konde's writing is a celebration of Cameroonian heritage and a testament to the power of words to bridge cultures and connect hearts.

For inquiries or collaborations, you can reach her at memoirekonde9@gmail.com.

Sacred Thread

By Tayong Hosea

In the heart of Africa, cradled by nature's hand,
Lies Cameroon, a country grand and in God's hand.
A triangular treasure of ten distinct regions,
Each boasting unique cultures and human legions.

Here, mosques and churches reach up towards the sky,
In collective adoration, their prayers do fly high.
A vibrant blend of tongues, where French and English meld,
A nation of 250 ethnic tongues, stories all upheld.

This land, where boundaries blur and hearts closely entwine,
With its mountains and valleys in most harmonious design.
Here, Mt. Cameroon stands tall, a guardian so bold,
Beside Lake Nyos and many forests, ancient and old.

Bountiful resources lie beneath its sparkling surface,
Ivory, gold, petroleum, in abundance, grace so generous.
Surrounded by neighbors, those near and those far,
Cameroon's grace shines like a bright guiding star.

A tranquil harmony weaves through this blessed nation,
As borders merge and we find our foundation.
Cameroon, where nature's grandeur unfolds at each turn,
A testament to the Creator's love, that in which we yearn.

In this vast land, ten regions proudly stand,
Each nurtured by nature's kind, gentle hand.
From Maroua's charm to Garoua's breeze,
Each city is a story, aimed truly to please.

Bertoua's gold gleams beneath the bright sun,
While Bamenda's climate offers respite and fun.
Douala's coastal beauty, Yaoundé's vibrant heart,
Each region plays its own unique part.

Together, they weave a pattern so wide and so grand,
A land of wonders, nature's firm and good hand.
In gratitude, we raise our voices on high
For Cameroon, all of us beneath God's vast blue sky.

In Cameroon's flag, the colors tell a tale
Of forests green, in unity, beneath sunlight pale.
From the mountains' majestic peaks,
To rainforests, where mystery speaks.

The land quakes, rivers flood, all shapes the terrain.
Nature's power shows its face in every drop of rain.

In this landscape, God's creativity shines truly through,
A biodiversity treasure, so bold and so true.

From the dense jungles, where wildlife roams free,
To the tranquil shores of Kribi and Limbe,
Agriculture thrives, mining uncovers great wealth,
In this land of diversity and spiritual health.

Among the Bakossi, the Bamiléké, and so many more,
Tribes rich in tradition, with cultures they adore,
Their dances and rhythms are expressions of joy,
A unity in diversity that nothing could destroy.

Our Christian faith is a bond that unites.
In churches, hymns fill even the darkest of nights.
Together, we stand, embracing our multiplicity,
In faith, culture, and in shared prosperity.
Yet, challenges arise, which cast some shadows of pain,
In the northwest and southwest, there are conflicts which strain.
We pray for peace, for wounds to be healed,
For unity and love to be the firm seal.

In darkness, hope remains our bright light,
The thing truly able to guide us through the night.
With compassion and love, we seek to rebuild
A land of peace, which by God's will is fulfilled.

So let us celebrate this blend of love,
Blessed by nature and the One God above.

In faith, culture, and nature, we find our strength.
For Cameroon, we would go to any length.

Together, in unity, we stand hand in hand,
Honoring our faith across our grand land.
Preserving our culture, our biodiversity we cherish,
With God as our guide, we will forever flourish.

In every heartbeat, in love's gentle embrace,
Cameroon's spirit, that which we forever chase.
A land woven with grace, its soul so divine,
In our Christian faith, culture, and nature, in that we intertwine.
Amen.

About the Author

Tayong Tayong Hosea is a budding educator and freelance writer, passionate about inspiring young minds and sharing his unique perspective through the written word. His dedication to teaching is evident in his commitment to continuous learning and his creative approach to education. As a freelance writer, Tayong explores diverse topics, from social commentary to personal reflections, always striving to engage and provoke thought.

Connect with Tayong at tayonghosea1995@gmail.com or follow his journey on Facebook (@Tayong Hosea) and Quora (Mr. Tayong Hosea) for thought-provoking content and insights into the world of education and writing.

Beyond the Veil: A Journey of Spirit and Truth

By Richard DEUGUEN TCHIAPI

(This article was originally submitted in French)

A wealthy and powerful man, seeking to end his wrongful deeds, pondered to himself, "How can I control everything, yet fail to control the evil I do? Surely, with willpower and moralism, I can become better."

Such thinking is absurdly flawed. We cannot improve while relying on the flesh alone, for the flesh is doomed to imperfection: "Those who are in the realm of the flesh cannot please God" (Romans 8:8). Carnal beings (those driven by will, morality, desire, etc.) cannot replace the spiritual being and can only totally surrender to God. Returning to God is the only path to perfection (1 Peter 5:10).

Paul, known as Saul before his conversion to Christ, zealously persecuted Jesus Christ, as he lived solely by human law. This led him to disdain, oppress, and deprive many, even to the point of approving of death. He sought the law's perfection, but on the road to Damascus, he encountered the perfection of love: Jesus Christ (Acts 22:3-21). His heart was transformed. His name became Paul, and everything became new for him (2 Corinthians 5:17); he became the apostle to the Gentiles. Free your hearts from the emblems that make them insensitive to love. Like Paul, let the Prince of Peace, Jesus Christ, touch you.

Your life is precious (Isaiah 43:3-7). Some may say it's worthless but nothing can ever truly equal its value. Do not boast of it either, for it is too short. No one of us may believe ourself more powerful, intelligent, beautiful, wealthy, or better than anyone else. Do not lose sight of what truly matters by making such mistakes. These things we have are things many have possessed, but what of those people now? Death is insatiable. If you are unsure what should hold utmost importance in your life, you are an unfulfilled being.

Saul was so handsome that the Bible asserts no Israelite was more beautiful than him (1 Samuel 9:2). Chosen by God as King of Israel, his disobedience then led him to madness and a miserable death (1 Samuel 15-31). His kingdom was given to a poor shepherd named David, a man after God's own heart (Acts 13:22). Before assigning value to anything in your life, know there is nothing new under the sun (Ecclesiastes 1:9).

"When we are born, we are old enough to die" (Heidegger). God created you with reason and conscience, for "reason and conscience are the infallible guides to good and evil that make Man akin to God" (Rousseau). Are you akin to God? If not, change today. You are always old enough to die.

Death will not consider who you are or what you have. Your life appears for a little while and then vanishes entirely (James 4:14). What purpose would it have served if it ended today? What memories would you leave in the hearts of those who love you? What truth would they know of you?

Do you love people for who they are, for what they have, for what they give? Or do you trade a little love for a bit of what they offer? Are others merely objects for your enjoyment? Why do you always harbor the thought of taking advantage of others? Does your life hold more value than another's? Do the pains you've suffered give you the right to inflict suffering? If life offered the same advantages and opportunities to everyone, many would be surprised by their current lives. You must love your neighbor! Yes, love them. Put yourself in their place and have for them the same consideration you would for yourself (Mark 12:31).

Be assured, whatever life or lives you lead, they will be buried with you, not with the consequences they generate. These consequences are what will remain. You will leave this earth as you came. However, you will be well-dressed and placed between four well-treated, even personalized pieces of wood, measured by your wealth. Do not be deceived. Nothing in this world is eternal, except love (1 Corinthians 13:8).

I know, if death could be bribed, some would live forever. But if Man was assured of inheriting a kingdom as a reward after death, the Earth would already be devoid of its inhabitants. Death is inevitable, and you are 100% eligible. You will be sent there.

Throughout our lives, only three days are important: yesterday, today, and tomorrow. Yesterday is a recent or distant past whose knowledge is now very clear to us, while tomorrow is an unknown future, full of projects whose fulfillment depends on a will superior to our own. Let's see today as an opportunity to correct yesterday and to perfect tomorrow, relying only on God.

Lost in this era of emptiness, in the derision of axiological relativism and social influence, we lose the sense of values intrinsic to humanity. We devote our existence to unbridled greed, witchcraft, arrogance, corruption, theft, fornication, adultery, lying, cheating, etc. It is imperative that every person return to their Creator with all their being. We must be focused on the only perfect model and reference: Jesus Christ, by whom every spirit is sharpened. We must live according to the spirit and not to the desires of the flesh (Galatians 5:16-26).

==

About the Author

Richard Deuguen Tchiapi is a biomedical sciences student at the University of Dschang, Cameroon. Passionate about reading, art, and science, Richard seeks to understand the complexities of life through both academic study and creative expression. An active member of the Christian Missionary Fellowship International, he shares his insights and experiences on Facebook at Richard Deug.

For inquiries or collaborations, you can reach him at richarddeuguen@gmail.com.

Unity in Diversity: Enanga's Crosscultural Legacy

By Ngayer Silvie T

Enanga emerged from the bustling Yaoundé Nsimalen International Airport, the familiar scent of roasted plantains and diesel fumes a stark contrast to the crisp Canadian air she had grown accustomed to. Her heart pounded with a mix of excitement and trepidation as she prepared to re-enter the world she had left behind four years ago.

Her parents, Mr. and Mrs. Tekapso, stood eagerly in the crowd. Mr. Tekapso, a tall, imposing figure with a gentle smile, was a respected scholar of African languages, his love for his Bafoussam heritage evident in his every word and gesture. Mrs. Tekapso, affectionately known as "OvenGuru," was a whirlwind of energy, her infectious laughter and entrepreneurial spirit the driving force behind her thriving bakery in Ngola. They had raised Enanga to embrace both her Anglophone and Francophone roots, a bilingual upbringing that had served her well in Canada.

The journey home had been a blur of emotions. Enanga's academic triumphs in Canada had filled her with pride, but news of her father's accident had cast a dark cloud over her homecoming. As she embraced her parents, their familiar scents and warmth washing over her, a pang of guilt pierced her heart. Had she been too focused on her own ambitions, neglecting the people who mattered most?

As they drove from the airport, her mother's voice broke the heavy silence, threading through the hum of the car. "You know, your father talked about your graduation every day. He had this whole celebration planned out in his mind," she said, her voice a mix of pride and sorrow.

Enanga nodded, feeling the weight of the moment, "I wish he could have been there, Mom. It was all for him—"

Her father cut in, his voice steady yet thick with unshed tears, "He was so proud, Enanga. We both are. You've become everything we dreamed of and more."

The car fell silent again, but the words hung in the air, painting Enanga's achievements with a bittersweet tinge. She glanced out the window, the familiar landscape now a tapestry of memories and dreams, each mile closer to home weaving her past with her present.

When they arrived at their home in Ngola, the lack of the usual boisterous welcome was palpable. The house, usually buzzing with the sounds of laughter and chatter, was eerily quiet. Her mother, with a somber expression, led her to the backyard where the reality of her father's absence was unmistakably clear—a freshly dug grave lay beneath the mango tree he had planted years ago. Enanga collapsed to her knees, overwhelmed by a torrent of grief.

In the days that followed, Enanga immersed herself in her father's belongings, seeking solace in the familiar scent of his old books and the faded ink of his handwritten notes. Tucked between the pages of his favorite novel, she found a letter addressed to her. With trembling hands, she unfolded the crinkled paper, her eyes blurring with tears as she read his final words.

"My dearest Enanga," the letter began, his elegant handwriting a poignant reminder of his gentle spirit. "My heart swells with pride as I reflect on your accomplishments. You have always been a beacon of light, a source of joy in my life. Even though my time on this earth has been cut short, I have no regrets. I have lived a full and meaningful life, surrounded by the love of my family and community.

"Remember, my dear daughter, that your roots run deep in this land. Embrace your heritage, cherish your bilingualism, and use your knowledge to uplift those around you. Never forget the lessons we taught you, the importance of hard work, integrity, and compassion. And most importantly, never lose faith in God's plan for your life.

"As I embark on my next journey, know that my love for you will always be with you. You are my greatest legacy, the embodiment of all my hopes and dreams. Go forth, my dear Enanga, and shine your light upon the world."

Enanga clutched the letter to her chest, tears streaming down her face. Her father's words echoed in her mind, a guiding light in her darkest hour. She knew that she could not let her grief consume her. She had a mission to fulfill, a legacy to uphold.

With renewed determination, Enanga channeled her grief into action. She returned to her studies, earning a master's degree in journalism and embarking on a career that would take her to the forefront of Cameroonian media. Her bilingual reporting, infused with her unique cultural perspective, resonated with audiences across the country. She became a voice for the voiceless, a champion of truth and justice.

Enanga's success extended beyond her professional life. She generously provided for her mother, ensuring that she lived comfortably and without worry. She mentored aspiring journalists, sharing her knowledge and experience with the next generation. And within her church community, she found love, a love that echoed the deep affection and respect shared by her parents.

Enanga's wedding, a vibrant celebration of Cameroonian culture, was a testament to the unity she embodied. As she danced with her husband, surrounded by the love and laughter of her family and friends, she knew that her journey had come full circle. She had found her place in the world, a place where her two identities, her two languages, her two cultures, could coexist in harmony.

Her story is a testament to the power of perseverance, the importance of embracing one's heritage, and the enduring strength of the human spirit. Enanga's life is a beacon of hope, a reminder that even in the face of adversity, we can rise above our circumstances and create a brighter future for ourselves and those we love.

About the Author

Mrs. Ngayer Silvie T. is a passionate English teacher dedicated to empowering her students with language skills and cultural understanding. She extends her reach beyond the classroom through engaging social media content on Facebook (Ngayer Silvie Epse Talikong), Instagram (@Sil_nk.best), and TikTok (SpeakEnglishWithSilvie), where she shares language tips, cultural insights, and inspirational messages.

For inquiries or collaborations, you can reach her at silvietalikong765@gmail.com.

Aïssatou's Path from Adversity to Hope

By Nguele Mbeng Justine

(This article was originally submitted in French)

The familiar scent of woodsmoke and spices hung heavy in the air, a reminder of home that twisted into a knot of anxiety in my stomach. "Make yourself beautiful and wear your finest dress, Aïssatou," commanded Djibril, my elder brother, his voice as cold and sharp as the desert wind.

My fingers tightened around the worn pages of my cherished book. "Who's visiting today?" I asked, my voice barely above a whisper. Djibril was a man of few words and even fewer visitors.

"Mr. Ahmadou and some associates," he replied curtly.

Just hearing his name sent a chill down my spine. Mr. Ahmadou was a wealthy herdsman, known in our village not just for his riches but for his harshness and his eye for young brides. I stood slowly, my legs shaking beneath me.

"Is there a problem?" Djibril eyed me, a hint of suspicion in his gaze.

"No," I lied, my voice hoarse.

"Then hurry up and do as you're told," he snapped, taking the book from my hands with a dismissive gesture. "You worry too much."

Reluctantly, I retreated to my room. It was small, with just enough space for my few belongings. The mirror was cracked but it reflected my transformation as I adorned myself in a vibrant boubou and silver jewelry that felt like shackles against my skin.

Emerging from my room, I caught Djibril's sorrowful glance. His face softened for just a moment before an authoritative voice called from outside, "Djibril...!"

"Are we in trouble?" I whispered, sensing the tension in the air.

"No," he mouthed silently, his attention now fixed on the door.

Mr. Ahmadou entered, his imposing figure overshadowing the modest furnishings of our living space. He slumped onto the sofa, which creaked under his weight.

"I'm here for my money," he stated bluntly, his voice a deep rumble.

Color drained from Djibril's face. "I don't have it, sir. But hear me out, I have another offer..."

My heart pounded in my chest, foreboding filling me as I realized what was about to happen.

"This is Aïssatou, my sister," Djibril's voice broke as he gestured towards me. "She can settle the debt."

I gasped, my voice stuck in my throat as I struggled to speak.

Mr. Ahmadou stood, his height dominating the small room as he circled me, appraising me like livestock. My eyes filled with tears, my body frozen in place.

"She's young, beautiful, fertile," Djibril added, his voice emotionless as if he were discussing a business transaction.

"Indeed," Mr. Ahmadou mused, pausing to look me over. "But her youth..."

"She's well-behaved, won't cause you any trouble," Djibril cut in quickly, his voice eager, almost desperate.

I mustered the little courage I had. "Please, don't do this," I whispered, tears streaming down my face.

But it was as if I hadn't spoken.

"Deal's done," Mr. Ahmadou declared firmly. "You owe me nothing now, Djibril."

In that moment, I felt reduced to nothing more than a means to settle a debt. The years that followed were a blur of hardship and degradation in Mr. Ahmadou's household, each day a battle against his tyrannical rule. My dreams of studying and healing the sick seemed forever out of reach.

One evening, under the vast, starry sky, I sat outside, watching my son Ibrahim play. Something within me stirred—a fierce determination. I would not let my spirit be crushed. I whispered a promise to myself and to him, "We will be free."

The chance came when Mr. Ahmadou left on a lengthy trip. Seizing the opportunity, I took Ibrahim, and with nothing but a small bag, we fled into the night. Our journey was arduous, through unforgiving landscapes and under the scorching sun, until we reached the bustling streets of Douala.

There, life was tough, but I found work and saved every coin, each day fueled by the dream of returning to school. With time, determination, and the support of kind souls who believed in me, I made it into medical school. It was a grueling path, but my resolve never wavered.

Now, as a doctor, I look back on those dark days with a bittersweet pride. I achieved not just for myself, but for my son and for every girl who dares to dream amidst despair. My journey is a testament to the resilience of the human spirit, a beacon of hope for those still fighting for their dreams.

About the Author

Nguele Mbeng Justine is a dedicated educator pursuing a Master's degree while generously volunteering her time to teach English in high schools. Her passion for language and education shines through her commitment to shaping the minds of future generations. With a focus on fostering a love for learning and empowering students to reach their full potential, Justine is making a lasting impact on her community.

To connect with Justine and learn more about her inspiring journey, you can reach her at justinenguele7@gmail.com.

The Melody of Benjamin's Faith

By FAKA LOÏS FLEUR

(This article was originally submitted in French)

In the vibrant heart of Garoua, a city cradled in Northern Cameroon's embrace, the rhythm of Benjamin Kalgong's dual life resonated deeply. Known affectionately as "Benji" to friends and students alike, he navigated the labyrinth of knowledge as a respected teacher by day. Yet, beneath this facade of tranquility, a deeper melody stirred within him—a profound yearning to share his music beyond the church walls, to reach across Cameroon's diverse landscapes and touch countless souls.

Despite the allure of his dream, the comforting melody of security—the steady income from teaching—held him back from stepping into the uncertainty of a full-time music career.

One fateful evening, under the sprawling branches of an ancient baobab tree—a silent witness to generations of his family's joys and sorrows—Benji felt the unmistakable stirrings of destiny. The whispers of his calling grew into a chorus, compelling him to embrace the less traveled path.

Compelled by a blend of trepidation and excitement, he bid farewell to his life in Garoua. Before leaving, he stood in his empty classroom one last time, running his fingers over the well-worn desks, a tangible farewell to his old life, a life filled with routine and reassurance now being left behind.

Arriving in Ngaoundéré, a city known for its melodic diversity and cultural tapestry, Benji faced new challenges and opportunities. He joined the Siloé assembly, a modest church in the bustling Mbiden neighborhood. Amidst a congregation speaking in the musical tones of Mundang, Gbaya, and Mbum, Benji found a new home and purpose.

As days turned into weeks, the stark reality of his financial situation settled in. His meager earnings as a musician barely covered the cost of a single meal. The once-full cupboards in his small apartment grew bare, echoing his growling stomach. Each clink of a coin in his pocket was a stark reminder of the sacrifices he had made, a cold weight settling in the pit of his stomach as he skipped meals to make ends meet.

During this time of hardship, Benji found kinship in the Cameshe, a group of young worshippers bound by their shared love for music and faith. Among them were Déon, a wise artisan whose quiet strength often guided the group; Lisse, a nursing student whose voice could soothe the weariest of hearts, often sharing tales of her challenging hospital shifts; and Becca, whose infectious laughter and spontaneity brought light to their darkest moments.

Together, they created a sanctuary of faith and fellowship. In Benji's cramped apartment, they held impromptu jam sessions, filling the modest space with music that transcended their physical confines. These moments, rich with camaraderie and shared struggles, became a lifeline for Benji.

One evening, as they shared a simple meal of rice and beans, Déon addressed Benji's growing despair with a gentle firmness. "My brother," he said, his eyes reflecting deep empathy, "you cannot pour from an empty cup. It might be wise to find a small job, something to sustain you while you continue to pursue your calling."

Benji's pride bristled at the suggestion, but the truth in Déon's words was undeniable. He took up a job at Buberon, a dimly lit bar where the music clashed sharply with the sacred hymns he cherished. The raucous laughter and clinking glasses felt alien, yet he persevered, his voice a mere shadow of its former glory.

One tumultuous night at Buberon, as Benji's voice struggled to rise above the din, Belle, his friend from the Cameshe, appeared out of the shadows. Her face, a mix of sadness and concern, mirrored his own internal turmoil. "Benji," she whispered urgently over the noise, "is this truly the path you meant to follow?"

Her words pierced the fog of his resignation. Filled with a renewed sense of purpose, he left the bar that night, his mind racing with thoughts of his true calling as he wandered through the rain-soaked streets of Ngaoundéré.

The following morning, as Benji navigated his motorcycle through the blinding rain, a sudden skid sent him careening into the path of an oncoming car. The impact shattered his body, a searing pain engulfing him as he was thrown through the air. He landed with a sickening crunch, the world dissolving into a kaleidoscope of fragmented images and muffled sounds before succumbing to a darkness that mirrored his despair.

Lying in a hospital bed, visions of celestial realms—a glimpse into the divine—both awed and admonished him. He witnessed the ethereal beauty of paradise, where harmonious melodies and radiant lights filled the air, and the torments of a dark abyss, where despair and cacophony overwhelmed the senses. These visions were stark reminders of the path he was meant to follow.

When he returned to the world of the living, it was with a spirit transformed. Embracing his ministry with renewed vigor, his voice now carried a power that transcended previous limits. The Cameshe welcomed him back, their bond fortified by the trials they had endured.

Together, they embarked on a new journey. Their divine mission to spread music and faith resonated across Cameroon, their harmonies a beacon of light in a world yearning for salvation. As they performed in village squares and city centers, the faces of their audience—lit with hope and touched by grace—reflected the profound impact of their mission, a testament to the transformative power of faith and the enduring human spirit.

==

About the Author

Faka Loïs Fleur is a talented Cameroonian event decorator specializing in creating unforgettable atmospheres for weddings, birthdays, and conferences. With a passion for design and a keen eye for detail, Loïs works closely with clients to bring their visions to life, ensuring each event is a unique and personalized experience. Her creativity and dedication to customer satisfaction have made her a sought-after decorator in the region.

To discuss your event decor needs and explore Loïs's exquisite designs, you can connect with her on Facebook as "Loïs Fleur" or via email at lfakadejesus@gmail.com.

Saved by Faith

By DONG A NWATCHOCK DIMITRI BAUDOIN

(This article was originally submitted in French)

"But Jesus said to the woman, 'Your faith has saved you; go in peace.'" - Luke 7:50

My earliest memories are not of parents, but of the warm embrace of Caritas Orphanage in the bustling neighborhood of Nkolmesseng, Yaoundé. We were a motley crew of twenty-five children, each with our own story of loss, yet bound together by a shared hope for a better future. We lacked material wealth, but our lives were rich in the currency of prayer, sharing, forgiveness, humility, and above all, faith. These were the cornerstones upon which our caregivers, our earthly angels, built our lives.

The orphanage was a vibrant tapestry of childhood joys—shared meals, laughter echoing through the halls, and lessons learned not just from books but from life itself. I thrived in this environment, and my academic journey took me to the Bilingual High School of Essos. In 2015, I achieved a milestone, passing my Baccalauréat A4 Spanish. Yet, with this triumph came uncertainty about the future.

After much soul-searching, the pull towards teaching became undeniable. It resonated with my love for sharing knowledge, leading me to enroll at the University of Yde1 for a degree in languages. My journey continued at the ENS, the Higher Teacher Training College, where I aspired to shape young minds as a General Secondary Education Teacher.

By the grace of God, I navigated this path with determination and success. Three years later, I graduated, and the following year, I was accepted into the competitive ENS program. I shared this joy with my orphanage family, their elation reflecting my own.

To support myself, I balanced a part-time job at a quaint bookstore in Bastos with running an online business selling men's clothing and shoes. The early days were challenging, with sales barely trickling in. Doubt often gnawed at my resolve, but my mantra, "Start small and aim big," kept me steadfast. My efforts gradually began to bear fruit, with orders steadily increasing and customers becoming loyal patrons, spreading the word about my business. My network expanded, and soon, I had two young employees assisting me.

Despite my burgeoning success, I never lost touch with my roots. Regular visits to the orphanage were my anchor, offering support and guidance to the children who now filled the rooms I once called home.

Upon graduating from ENS, I was assigned to the Lycée de Manengouba in Nkongsamba, a town steeped in rich traditions and surrounded by the lush landscapes of Moungo. Eager to give back, I brought along a younger sister from the orphanage, committed to providing her with the opportunities I had been given.

However, my new life took a sinister turn. Nightmares plagued me, filled with shadowy figures from the community, their eyes accusing, their voices whispering threats. Each morning, I'd find unsettling objects—fetishes, bones, cryptic symbols—on my doorstep and even on my desk at school. A cold dread settled over me, transforming my once peaceful nights into battlegrounds of fear.

The more I prayed for protection, the more intense the attacks became. One evening, as a bone-chilling cold seeped into my very marrow, I stumbled through my door, barely coherent. My sister's worried gaze met mine. "You're here," she whispered, "but not really here." Her voice was the last thing I heard before darkness claimed me.

I awoke in the District Hospital of Nkongsamba, my body a frail husk, the bones stark beneath my skin. A battery of tests yielded no answers. In a hushed conversation with the doctor, I poured out my fears and the torment I had endured. His diagnosis was swift and chilling: "Your affliction is not of the body, but of the spirit."

Retreating to my home, too weak to teach, the days blurred into a haze of fevered dreams and sleepless nights. A local priest became my beacon of hope, guiding me through daily prayer sessions. My sister, my steadfast caregiver, shielded me with her unwavering love and prayers.

As the community learned of my plight, my students and fellow teachers rallied around me, their faces etched with concern. Their prayers, whispered fervently around my bed, were a balm to my wounded spirit. Amidst the darkness, a soft yet resolute voice whispered within me, "Hold on. You will be well again."

Clinging to that sliver of hope, I prayed with a fervor I had never known. Slowly, the darkness receded. Strength returned to my limbs, and the nightmares that had haunted me faded into distant echoes. After three months of agony, I emerged healed, my faith deeper and more profound than ever.

Prayer, the language of my faith, had indeed saved me. "I have set the Lord always before me; because he is at my right hand, I shall not be shaken." - Psalm 16:8.

Returning to teaching, I now carry a new understanding of the trials and tribulations we face. Each day in the classroom, I share not just academic knowledge, but lessons in resilience and faith, inspired by my journey. As I teach, I see the reflection of my own story in the eager eyes of my students—a testament to the transformative power of faith and the enduring human spirit.

About the Author

Dimitri Baudoin is a Cameroonian cultural entrepreneur and the visionary founder of "Le pkwem," a clothing and cultural brand that celebrates Cameroonian heritage. Through "Le pkwem," Dimitri and his team promote art, fashion, and social initiatives like "Un enfant-Un avenir," empowering vulnerable youth with essential skills. He also offers project management services for social, cultural, and creative projects, contributing to a vibrant cultural landscape. With a background in sales, copywriting, and dance, and currently leading the University of Douala's fan club, Dimitri is a multifaceted talent who believes in the boundless potential of youth.

Email: dimitridong5@gmail.com
Facebook (Le pkwem)
Twitter (Dong Dimitri)

www.ingramcontent.com/pod-product-compliance
Lightning Source LLC
LaVergne TN
LVHW010614110826
845149LV00003B/907

* 9 7 9 8 9 9 0 7 1 6 5 0 6 *